W9-CMZ-858

South Haven Public Library
403 West 700 North
Valparaiso, IN 46385

Porter County Public Library

South Haven Public Library
403 West 700 North
Valparaiso, IN 46385

sjbfi SH
BEECH

Beechen, Adam, author
Who is the Question?
33410013652583 11/24/15

STONE ARCH BOOKS
a capstone imprint

STONE ARCH BOOKS™

Published in 2013
A Capstone Imprint
1710 Roe Crest Drive
North Mankato, MN 56003
www.capstonepub.com

Originally published by DC Comics in the U.S. in single magazine form as Justice League Unlimited #8.
Copyright © 2013 DC Comics. All Rights Reserved.

DC Comics
1700 Broadway, New York, NY 10019
A Warner Bros. Entertainment Company

No part of this publication may be reproduced in whole or in part, or stored in a retrieval system, or transmitted in any form or by any means, electronic, mechanical, photocopying, recording, or otherwise, without written permission.

Printed in China by Nordica.
0413/CA21300442
032013 007226NORDF13

Cataloging-in-Publication Data is available at the Library of Congress website:
ISBN: 978-1-4342-6044-4 (library binding)

Summary: The Question's convinced there's a mind-controlled traitor in the Justice League and sets out to investigate. Of course, no one on the team takes him seriously. Can he get to the bottom of the mystery before the League's secrets are compromised?

STONE ARCH BOOKS

Ashley C. Andersen Zantop *Publisher*
Michael Dahl *Editorial Director*
Sean Tulien & Donald Lemke *Editors*
Heather Kindseth *Creative Director*
Bob Lentz & Hilary Wacholz *Designers*
Kathy McColley *Production Specialist*

DC COMICS

Tom Palmer Jr. *Original U.S. Editor*

JUSTICE LEAGUE UNLIMITED

WHO IS THE QUESTION?

Adam Beechen.. writer
Carlo Barberi & Walden Wong.................artists
Heroic Age ....colorist
Phil Balsman...letterer

JUSTICE
LEAGUE
UNLIMITED

I'M THE QUESTION.
AND I WANT ANSWERS.

NORMALLY, I WORK ALONE, AND THAT'S THE WAY I LIKE IT. I WON'T RELY ON ANYONE, AND I DON'T TRUST ANYONE.
BUT WHEN THE JUSTICE LEAGUE ASKED ME TO JOIN THEIR RANKS, I HAD TO SAY YES...
...THEY'D HAVE BEEN SUSPICIOUS OF ME IF I HADN'T.
THE LEAGUE IS AN ORGANIZATION OF INCREDIBLY POWERFUL SUPERHEROES DEDICATED TO PROTECTING ALL THINGS GOOD AND FREE FROM TITANIC, WORLD-SHATTERING EVIL MENACES.
THEY'RE VERY GOOD AT DEFEATING THE BIG, OBVIOUS THREATS...
...BUT SOMETIMES, THE LITTLE DETAILS CAN SLIP THROUGH THE CRACKS.

THE JUSTICE LEAGUE IS BASED IN A SERIES OF WATCHTOWER SATELLITES RINGED AROUND EARTH.
ONCE A WEEK, WE COME TOGETHER FOR A FULL MEMBERSHIP MEETING.
THE JUSTICE LEAGUE HAS A LOT OF ENEMIES, SOME OF THEM VERY SNEAKY.
SO ONCE A WEEK, I PATROL THE VENTILATION SHAFTS OF ALL THE WATCHTOWER SATELLITES. JUST IN CASE.
TODAY, I FOUND THIS.
I DON'T KNOW WHAT IT IS, BUT I CAN'T SHAKE THE FEELING THE DESIGN IS FAMILIAR.
IT WAS SET TO A TIMER, SUPPOSED TO GO OFF DURING OUR MEETING.
LUCKY I FOUND IT AND DEACTIVATED IT.

NOT KNOWING WHO PLANTED THE DEVICE, I CAN'T TELL MY TEAMMATES...
...IT MIGHT HAVE BEEN ONE OF THEM.
SEVERAL OF THE LEAGUE'S FOES ARE MIND-CONTROLLERS, AND THEY MIGHT STILL BE CONTROLLING THEIR UNWILLING ACCOMPLICE.
OTHER ENEMIES CAN BECOME INVISIBLE, OR THEY'RE SHAPE-CHANGERS, SO AFTER PLANTING THE DEVICE, THEY MIGHT HAVE STAYED ON THE WATCHTOWER. THEY COULD OVERHEAR ME VOICING MY SUSPICIONS...
SO IT'S BEST TO KEEP THIS TO MYSELF FOR THE MOMENT...
...UNTIL I'VE HAD THE CHANCE TO ASK THE RIGHT QUESTIONS.
JFK

MY TEAMMATES LOOK AT ME FUNNY. BECAUSE I KEEP TO MYSELF. I KNOW IT'S BETTER THAT WAY.
THEY DON'T UNDERSTAND. THEY THINK I'M A CONSPIRACY NUT. PARANOID.
UFO'S
SOMETIMES I WONDER IF I AM.

BUT THEN I FIND SOMETHING LIKE THIS.

NERVE GAS. AND WHILE MY KNOWLEDGE OF SCIENCE IS PRETTY BASIC, THE COMPLICATED COMPOUND RINGS A BELL SOMEWHERE IN THE BACK OF MY MIND. BUT THAT'S NOT MY PROBLEM RIGHT NOW.
MY PROBLEM IS, THIS NERVE GAS IS FATAL TO HUMANS, KRYPTONIANS, MARTIANS, AND JUST ABOUT EVERYONE ELSE.

I'M LOOKING FOR SOMEONE WITH SCIENTIFIC KNOWLEDGE FOR SURE, STEALTH CAPABILITIES...
...OR PERHAPS TELEPATHIC DOMINATION OR MORPHING POWERS.

I HAVE A COMPUTER IN MY QUARTERS. I USE IT FOR INTRA-LEAGUE COMMUNICATION, CASUAL STUFF, BUT THAT'S ABOUT IT.
TOO EASY TO HACK.

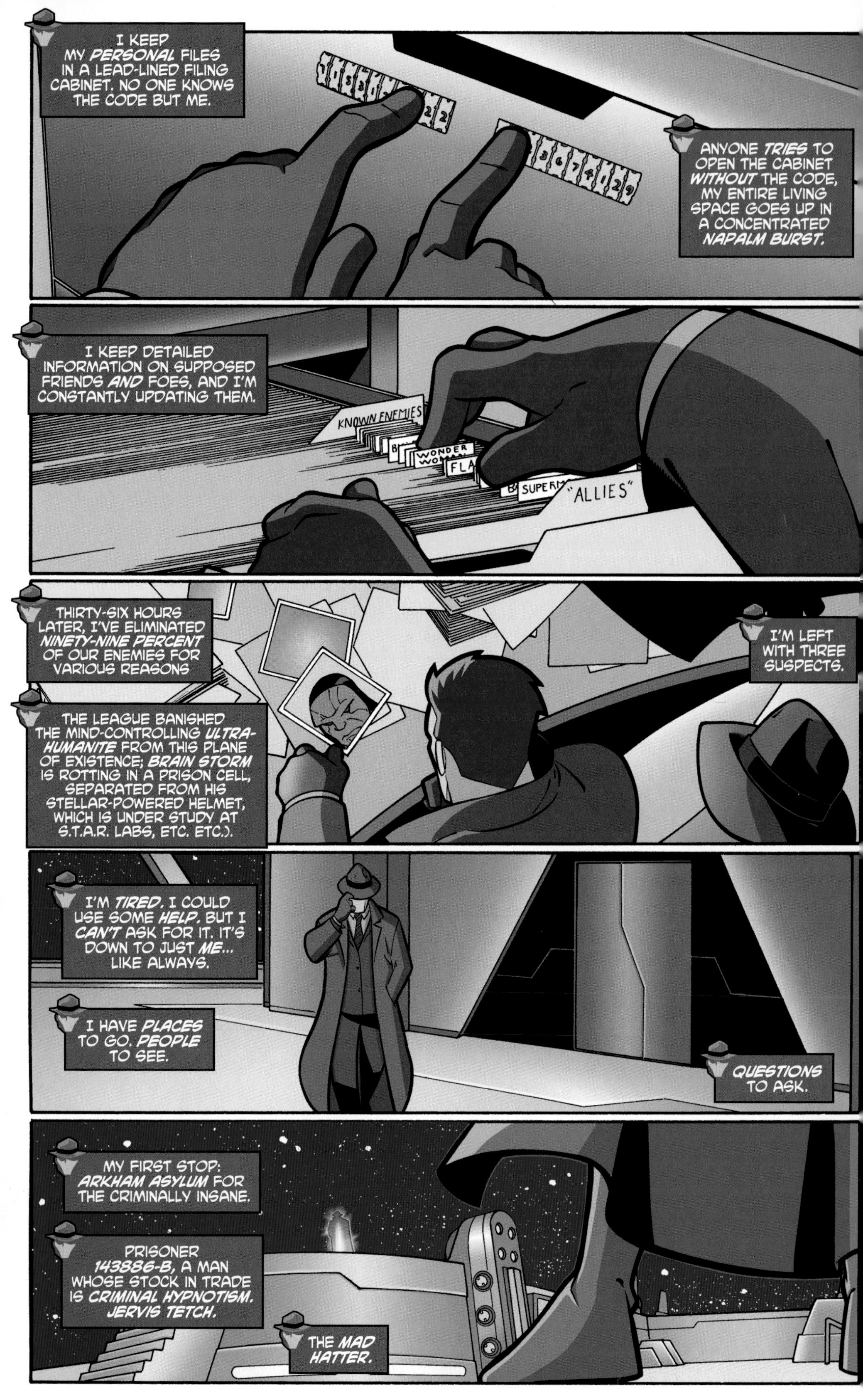

I KEEP MY PERSONAL FILES IN A LEAD-LINED FILING CABINET. NO ONE KNOWS THE CODE BUT ME.
ANYONE TRIES TO OPEN THE CABINET WITHOUT THE CODE, MY ENTIRE LIVING SPACE GOES UP IN A CONCENTRATED NAPALM BURST.
I KEEP DETAILED INFORMATION ON SUPPOSED FRIENDS AND FOES, AND I'M CONSTANTLY UPDATING THEM.
KNOWN ENEMIES
"ALLIES"
THIRTY-SIX HOURS LATER, I'VE ELIMINATED NINETY-NINE PERCENT OF OUR ENEMIES FOR VARIOUS REASONS
I'M LEFT WITH THREE SUSPECTS.
THE LEAGUE BANISHED THE MIND-CONTROLLING ULTRA-HUMANITE FROM THIS PLANE OF EXISTENCE; BRAIN STORM IS ROTTING IN A PRISON CELL, SEPARATED FROM HIS STELLAR-POWERED HELMET, WHICH IS UNDER STUDY AT S.T.A.R. LABS, ETC. ETC.).
I'M TIRED. I COULD USE SOME HELP. BUT I CAN'T ASK FOR IT. IT'S DOWN TO JUST ME... LIKE ALWAYS.
I HAVE PLACES TO GO. PEOPLE TO SEE.
QUESTIONS TO ASK.
MY FIRST STOP: ARKHAM ASYLUM FOR THE CRIMINALLY INSANE.
PRISONER 143886-B, A MAN WHOSE STOCK IN TRADE IS CRIMINAL HYPNOTISM. JERVIS TETCH.
THE MAD HATTER.

...TELL ME A STORY...
...FIRE DEATH BY FIRE DEATH BY FIRE DEATH BY...
HAHAH AHAHAHA HA...
YES IT DOES! NO IT DOESN'T! YES IT DOES!
...A BEAUTIFUL STORY ABOUT SAWS... AND RAZORS...
...FIRE DEATH BY FIRE DEATH BY FIRE DEATH BY...
HAHA HEHEHEHEHE HEEEE...
YOU DON'T KNOW WHAT YOU'RE TALKING ABOUT! OH, AND I SUPPOSE YOU DO?
143886-8
...EVERYONE CAN SEE WHAT I'M THINKING... CAN'T COVER MY THOUGHTS...
...PLEASE... LET ME HAVE A HAT, OR ALL MY THOUGHTS WILL FLY AWAY...
ONE SUSPECT DOWN, TWO TO GO.
...A TOP HAT, A TAM O'SHANTER, A BERET, OR EVEN A FEDORA...

THE QUESTION IS THIS: WHERE IS THE FIDDLER?
I... I... I DON'T KNOW!
WRONG ANSWER!
OO-OOOF!
THWHAMMM
WHOKK
THE FIDDLER: NOT THE BRIGHTEST OR BRAVEST OF THE LEAGUE'S FOES, BUT WHEN HE PLAYS HIS SPECIAL VIOLIN, HE CAN HYPNOTIZE OTHERS...
...AND MY FILES SAY HE'S AT LARGE.
SOMEWHERE, SOMEBODY KNOWS WHERE I CAN FIND HIM.
IT'S ONE OF THE TRUTHS OF THIS BUSINESS...
...THERE'S ALWAYS SOMEBODY WHO KNOWS.
SHAYNE'S! HE'S AT SHAYNE'S BAR! FIDDLER'S BEEN THERE EVERY NIGHT FOR THREE WEEKS!

SHAINE'S BAR
SCOTCH. AND LINE 'EM UP.
BAR & GRILL
YOU GOT IT, FIDDLER.

"FIDDLER." HA! NOT HARDLY. NOT SINCE I TRIED TO MOVE IN ON GIRDER'S TERRITORY...

HE GOT AHOLD OF ME AND TAUGHT ME A LESSON, ALL RIGHT...

HE MADE ME INTO JUST ANOTHER GUY DRINKING SCOTCH IN A BAR...

...THROUGH A STRAW.
TWO DOWN.

FIRED...? BUT SIR, THE LAST BREAK-IN ATTEMPT ON YOUR ESTATE--
--WAS TWELVE MINUTES AGO. AND IT WAS SUCCESSFUL, WASN'T IT...
WILL THERE BE ANYTHING ELSE, MR. LUTHOR?
YES. HAVE THE ENTIRE SECURITY TEAM FIRED IMMEDIATELY.
...QUESTION?
THAT REMAINS TO BE SEEN.
EEP!
AND HOW CAN I HELP MY FRIENDS IN THE JUSTICE LEAGUE?
DON'T GIVE ME THAT, LUTHOR. YOU MAY HAVE CONVINCED THE REST OF THE WORLD THAT YOU'VE GONE STRAIGHT...
...BUT I KNOW BETTER.
HMM, YOU'RE HERE BY YOURSELF, SO YOU MUST BELIEVE YOU CAN'T SHARE YOUR SUSPICIONS WITH YOUR TEAMMATES...
THEY SAY, "NO MAN IS AN ISLAND," BUT YOU'RE TRYING TO PROVE THAT WRONG, AREN'T YOU, QUESTION?
SOMEONE BREACHED WATCHTOWER DEFENSES AND PLANTED A DEVICE FILLED WITH NERVE GAS FATAL TO ALL RACES IN OUR VENTILATION SYSTEM.
SOMEONE WITH GENIUS...WITH SCIENTIFIC SKILL... AND PSYCHOPATHIC CUNNING.

WELL... THAT CERTAINLY SOUNDS LIKE ME...
...AND I DEFINITELY ADMIRE THE SCHEME...
...BUT I'M NOT THE PARTY RESPONSIBLE. NOR DO I KNOW WHO IS.
PROVE IT.
OH, I CAN'T. BUT THEN, I DON'T HAVE TO. "INNOCENT UNTIL PROVEN GUILTY," YOU KNOW.
AND LIKE YOU SAY...
...I'VE GONE STRAIGHT.
HURTING MY FRIENDS IN THE JUSTICE LEAGUE IS THE LAST THING ON MY MIND.
BUT IF I DID WANT TO DESTROY MY FORMER ENEMIES...
...AND YOU CAN TAKE THIS TO THE BANK...
...I'D WANT THEM TO KNOW IT WAS ME.
I DON'T TRUST HIM.
BUT I BELIEVE HIM.

I'VE MISSED SOMETHING.
IT WOULD HELP IF I COULD COMPARE NOTES WITH SOMEONE, BUT I DON'T DO THAT. IT'S NOT MY WAY.
UNANSWERED QUESTIONS LIKE THESE DRIVE ME CRAZY...
...PARTICULARLY WHEN I CAN'T SHAKE THE FEELING...
SSSKLITCH
...THE ANSWER IS RIGHT IN FRONT OF ME.

IN THE FIRST SECONDS OF ENGAGEMENT, I RUN DOWN IN MY MIND SOME OF THE ABILITIES OF THE MARTIAN MANHUNTER, AND SUDDENLY IT ALL SEEMS TO MAKE SENSE:
SHAPE-CHANGING.
KNOWLEDGE OF ALIEN SCIENCE AND TECHNOLOGY.
SENSITIVE TO TELEPATHY.
HE'S BEEN HYPNOTIZED.
AND THEN I REMEMBER THE SINGLE MARTIAN WEAKNESS...
...FIRE.
AAAAAARRRRGH!
NAPALM.
I KNEW IT WOULD COME IN HANDY.
QUESTION!

I'M NO MATCH FOR A HYPNOTIZED MARTIAN.
CERTAINLY NOT IN THESE CLOSE QUARTERS.
LISTEN TO ME! I AM NOT YOUR ENEMY!
YEAH, RIGHT.
HE SOUNDS LIKE HIMSELF, BUT I KNOW BETTER.
IF I'M LUCKY, I CAN MAKE IT DOWN TO METROPOLIS AND LOSE HIM...
IF I'M LUCKY, I'LL HAVE TIME TO MAKE SOME SORT OF PLAN...
SO MUCH FOR LUCK.
I KNOW WHAT YOU BELIEVE, BUT YOU ARE WRONG!
CLANG
CLANG
LET ME SHOW YOU!
HE'S TURNED INVISIBLE.
MARTIANS CAN DO THAT, TOO.
FOUND HIM.
WHUFF!

I'M GOING TO HAVE TO STAY IN CLOSE, TRY TO KEEP HIM FROM DISAPPEARING, TRY TO KEEP HIM OFF-BALANCE...
UNGH!
THWACK
...KEEP HIM FROM PULVERIZING ME.
THA BOOOM
QUESTION, STOP FIGHTING!
LET ME INTO YOUR MIND SO I CAN SHOW YOU THE TRUTH!
TRUST M-- HWUH?
NEVER! THE QUESTION TRUSTS NO ONE!
I'LL GO BACK TO THE WATCHTOWER, FIND WEAPONS STRONG ENOUGH TO DEFEAT HIM. THEN I'LL FIND THE ONES DOING THIS, AND--
NO!
SHWHAM
IT'S THE ONLY WAY I CAN MAKE YOU BELIEVE THE TRUTH, QUESTION, BUT I WON'T ENTER YOUR MIND UNLESS YOU LET ME!

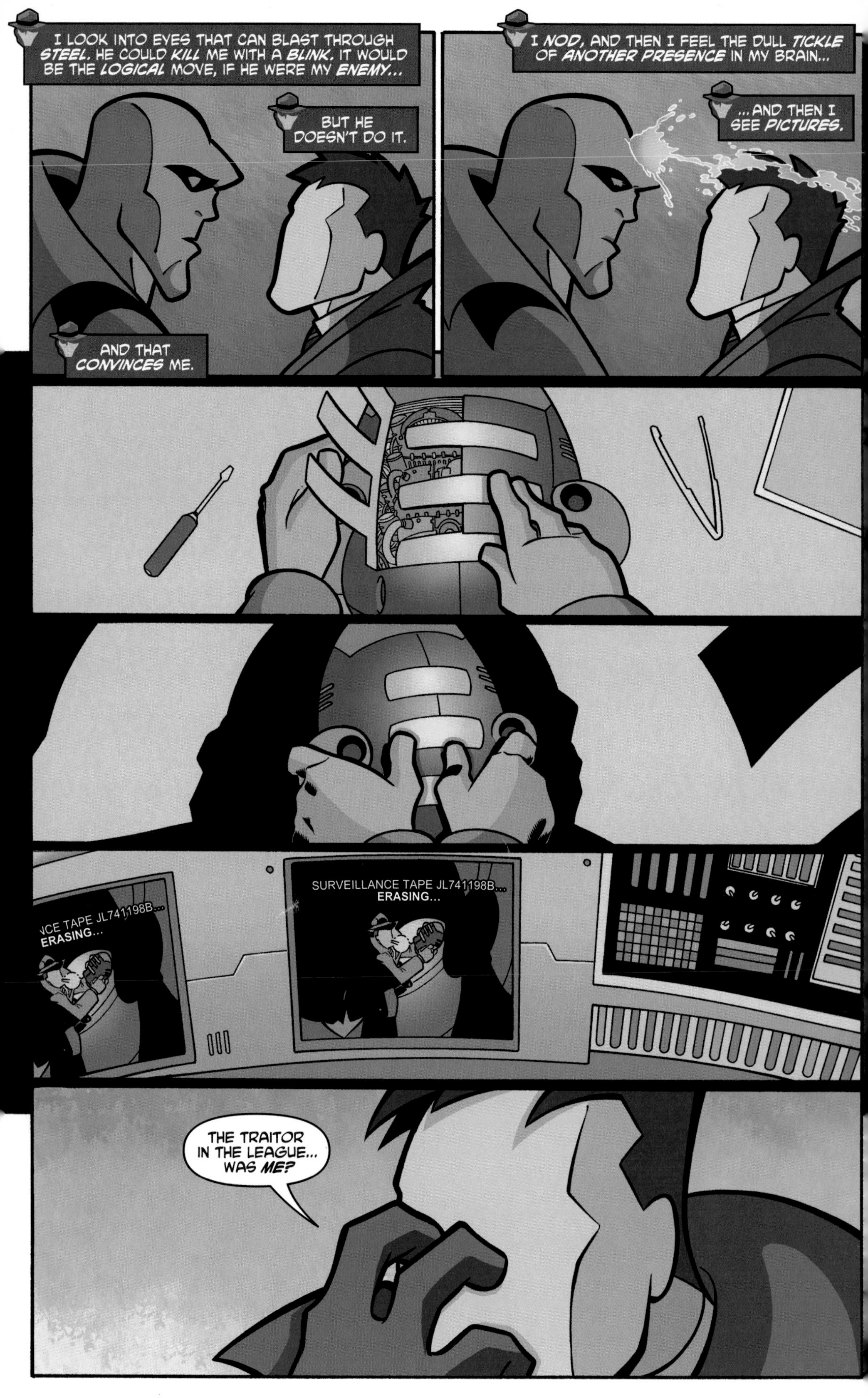
I LOOK INTO EYES THAT CAN BLAST THROUGH STEEL. HE COULD KILL ME WITH A BLINK. IT WOULD BE THE LOGICAL MOVE, IF HE WERE MY ENEMY...
BUT HE DOESN'T DO IT.
AND THAT CONVINCES ME.
I NOD, AND THEN I FEEL THE DULL TICKLE OF ANOTHER PRESENCE IN MY BRAIN...
...AND THEN I SEE PICTURES.
NCE TAPE JL741198B... ERASING...
SURVEILLANCE TAPE JL741198B... ERASING...
THE TRAITOR IN THE LEAGUE... WAS ME?

YES. YOU WERE *HYPNOTIZED* FROM LONG DISTANCE INTO CREATING AND PLANTING DEVICES THAT WOULD *DESTROY* THE ENTIRE LEAGUE.
I FOUND THIS *ELECTROMAGNETIC PULSE GENERATOR* IN YOUR QUARTERS JUST BEFORE YOU ENTERED. IT WAS TO BE YOUR NEXT *WEAPON.*
THAT'S WHY THE *DESIGNS*, THE *CHEMICALS*, LOOKED SO FAMILIAR...

I'D SENSED AN *UNIDENTIFIED TRANSMISSION* TO THE WATCHTOWER SEVERAL TIMES BEFORE, BUT WAS UNABLE TO IDENTIFY ITS *ENERGY SIGNATURE* OR ITS *DESTINATION.*
BUT THIS *LAST* TIME, DURING OUR MOST RECENT MEETING, I SENSED THE TRANSMISSION AT THE SAME TIME I HAPPENED TO SEE *YOU* ENTERING THE *VENTILATION SYSTEM.*

OBSERVING YOUR SUBSEQUENT CONFUSION, I DECIDED TO INVESTIGATE ON MY *OWN.*
AFTER FURTHER SCRUTINIZING THE *TRANSMISSIONS* TO DETERMINE THEIR *COMPOSITION,* I REALIZED THEY WERE CONNECTED TO YOUR *BEHAVIOR.*

GIVEN THAT, I EXAMINED REAL-TIME SECURITY VIDEO OF YOUR QUARTERS FROM WHEN YOU RETURNED FROM *ARKHAM ASYLUM.*
IT WAS CLEAR YOU WERE UNDER *PERIODIC HYPNOTIC CONTROL,* AND THAT *SELECTIVE MEMORY BLOCKS* HAD BEEN CREATED TO KEEP YOU FROM SEEING CERTAIN THINGS THAT WOULD ALERT YOU TO YOUR CONDITION.

IRONICALLY, YOUR SUSPICIOUS NATURE LED YOU TO *THWART* YOUR OWN EFFORTS...
...EVEN THOUGH YOU DID NOT REALIZE IT.

I'VE BEEN USED! BUT BY WHO?
WAIT, YOU SAID YOU IDENTIFIED THE COMPOSITION OF THE ENERGY TRANSMISSIONS INTO MY MIND...?
I HAVE...
...IT WAS STELLAR ENERGY.
"...DON'T KNOW WHY YOU'RE HERE, GENTLEMEN...WE HAD TROUBLE WITH HIM INITIALLY, BUT BRAIN STORM HAS BEEN A MODEL PRISONER FOR DAYS NOW..."
WITHOUT HIS STELLAR ENERGY HELMET, HE'S REALLY QUITE--
--OH, MY...
WE MAKE A QUICK STOP AT S.T.A.R. LABS TO CONFIRM OUR SUSPICIONS...
...MUST HAVE REPLACED IT SOMEHOW WITH A HOLOGRAM, BUT...?!

EH? MY HELMET CAN'T CONTACT THE QUESTION'S MIND...!
AND WHAT HAPPENED TO HIS QUARTERS...?
THE MANHUNTER PLACES TEMPORARY TELEPATHIC BARRIERS IN MY MIND SO BRAIN STORM CAN'T CONTROL ME AGAIN...

RRRRUUUNNCH
...AND THEN WE MAKE ANOTHER STOP AT THE JUSTICE LEAGUE WATCHTOWER...
EH?

...TO PICK UP SOME FRIENDS.

LATER, WITH BRAIN STORM SEPARATED FROM HIS HELMET AND RETURNED TO PRISON FOR GOOD, I REFLECT ON LUTHOR'S WORDS...
"NO MAN IS AN ISLAND."
I BELIEVED MY ISOLATION, MY UNWILLINGNESS TO TRUST, MY LACK OF FRIENDS, MADE ME STRONG...
INSTEAD, IT MADE ME A WEAK LINK, A PERFECT TARGET.
QUESTION...?
AM I GOING TO KEEP PLAYING IT THE WAY I ALWAYS HAVE? OR AM I GOING TO TAKE A CHANCE, SHOW SOME TRUST, AND LET PEOPLE IN ONCE IN A WHILE?
WOULD YOU LIKE SOME HELP?
I GUESS THAT'S THE QUESTION.
THE END

JUSTICE
LEAGUE
UNLIMITED

JUSTICE LEAGUE
UNLIMITED

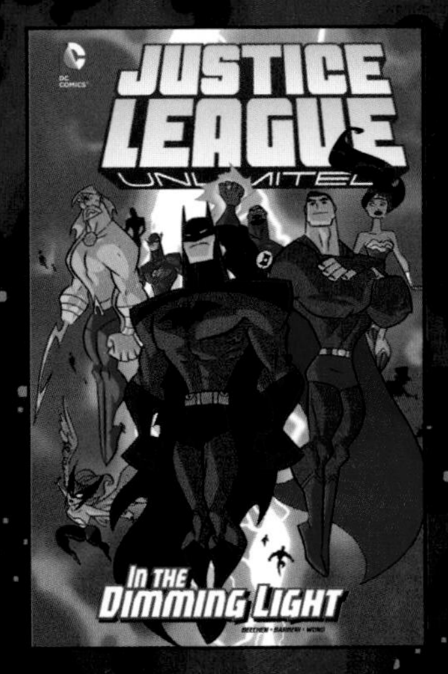

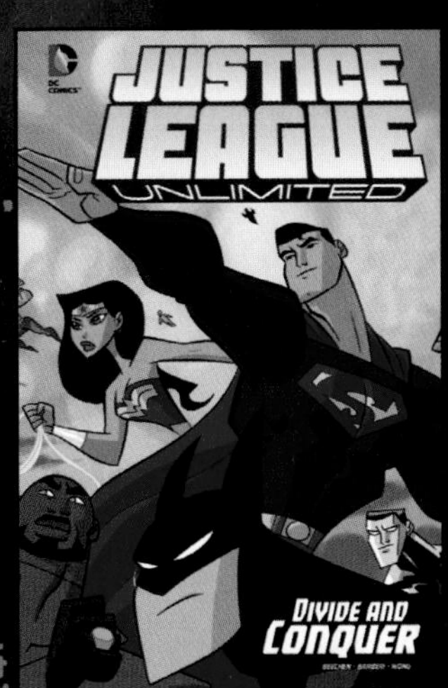

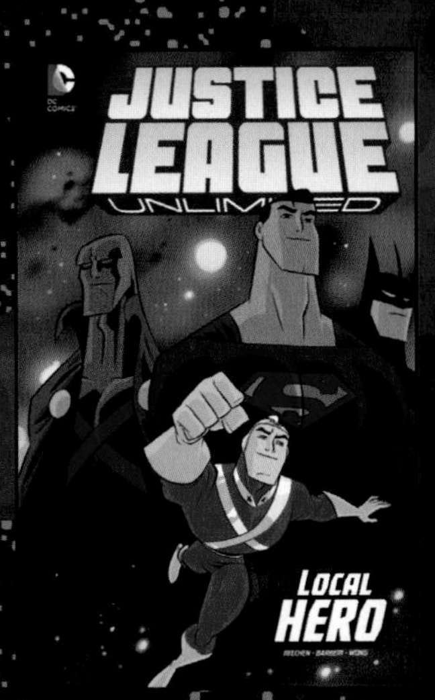

READ THEM ALL!

CREATORS

ADAM BEECHEN WRITER

Adam Beechen has written a variety of TV cartoons, including *Ben Ten: Alien Force, Teen Titans, Batman: The Brave and the Bold, The Batman* [for which he received an Emmy nomination], *Rugrats, The Wild Thornberrys, X-Men: Evolution,* and *Static Shock*, as well as the live-action series *Ned's Declassified School Survival Guide* and *The Famous Jett Jackson*. He is also the author of *Hench*, a graphic novel, and has scripted many comic books, including *Batgirl, Teen Titans, Robin,* and *Justice League Unlimited*. In addition Adam has written dozens of children's books, as well as an original young adult novel, *What I Did On My Hypergalactic Interstellar Summer Vacation*.

CARLO BARBERI ARTIST

Carlo Barberi is a professional comic book artist from Monterrey, Mexico. His best-known works for DC Comics include *Batman: The Brave and the Bold*, *The Flash*, *Blue Beetle*, *Gen 13*, and *Justice League Unlimited*.

WALDEN WONG ARTIST

Walden Wong is a professional comic book artist, inker, and colorist. He's worked on some of DC Comics' top characters, including Superman, Batman, Wonder Woman, and more.

WORD GLOSSARY

accomplice (uh-KOM-pliss)--someone who helps another person commit a crime

banished (BAN-ishd)--sent someone away from a place and ordered the person never to return

conspiracy (kuhn-SPEER-uh-see)--a secret, illegal plan made by two or more people

menaces (MEN-iss-iz)--threats or dangers, or people who are threatening and dangerous

napalm (NAY-pahm)--a highly flammable jellylike substance used as a weapon

psychopathic (sye-kuh-PATH-ik)--characteristic of a mental disease or insanity

subsequent (SUHB-see-kwuhnt)--coming after or following

suspicious (suh-SPISH-uhss)--if you feel suspicious, you think that something is wrong or bad but you have little or no proof to back up your feelings

telepathic (tel-uh-PATH-ik)--communication occurring from one mind directly to another

thwart (THWORT)--if you thwart somebody's plans, you prevent them from happening or succeeding

J.L.U. GLOSSARY

TELEPATHY

Martian Manhunter is able to read any human's mind. Only the minds of the mentally unstable can be difficult for him to read.

SHAPE-SHIFTING

Manhunter is also able to shift the shape of his body to anything that doesn't have moving parts.

MARTIAN VISION

Manhunter's vision gives him the ability to see invisible objects. It also allows him to use his eyes as weapons by sending out fiery blasts.

VISUAL QUESTIONS & PROMPTS

1. In this panel from page 14, what does Lex Luthor know that we don't yet know?

2. Why do you think the main character chose the super hero name "The Question" for himself?

3. By the end of this book, do you think the Question has changed? How? Read the last part of this book again for clues.

4. On page 21, a green hue has been added to several of the panels. Why did the creators of this comic book choose to apply this affect to certain panels and not others?

5. At what point in this story did you realize the Question was the one who planted the bomb? Identify the exact panel where you solved the mystery.

WANT EVEN MORE?

GO TO...

WWW.CAPSTONEKIDS.COM

Then find cool websites and more books like this one at *www.facthound.com.*

Just type in the BOOK ID:
9781434260444